Best Wishes
Steve Boyce

Cornelius Cone and Friends

It was early morning at the side of a quiet country road; the sound of a reversing highway maintenance truck was approaching, beeping and beeping as it neared a freshly repaired pothole, the truck then came to a stop with a loud ‘pshhhh’ of the brakes.

A short moment later, Cornelius Cone is dropped off onto the road.

‘There you go Cornelius, have a good day, we will pick you up later.’

The truck then drove away, like many traffic cones, Cornelius had a very important job to do, his bright reflective colours help warn motorists to keep clear of the newly repaired road surface.

Cornelius loved his job, he knew that it would also be very boring at times, he could be standing on the road day and night for weeks, but today, he was not given a flashing light to put on his head.

It was rare for Cornelius to be assigned to a country road, he was very excited, the countryside looked beautiful, the air was fresh, he smiled at a hedgehog and rabbit as they played on the grass, the birds were also singing a pleasant tune.

Soon, the sound of birdsong was lost in the noise of traffic; the road was beginning to get very busy, speeding wheels passed close to him, making him wobble.

Cornelius stood firm; he was used to this when he was working in a busy town.

'I am a sturdy bright and brave cone, what could go wrong? I can be seen a long way off.'

Before he could finish his sentence, a speeding car rushed close by, sending him flying off the road, up into the air and over the fence.

He landed with a thud on a steep grassy slope, rolling and rolling, bouncing and bouncing down the steep slope he rolled.

Rolling and rolling, bouncing and bouncing.

With a splash, he fell into a fast-flowing river.

Bobbing and bobbing, gasping and gasping, splishing and splashing he floated down the river.

The current was very strong, he struggled to keep his head above the water, he never required swimming lessons in the past, but as he was pulled helplessly by the strong current, he wished he had.

What seemed like a very long time in the river, he could see a shopping trolley in front of him; he crashed into the trolley.

‘Ouch, cried the trolly, watch where you’re going!’

‘Sorry, the current is very strong. I can’t swim.’ Replied Cornelius.

Cornelius quickly grabbed the trolley, pulling it down the river with him.

Eventually, in front of him was a fallen tree, Cornelius managed to grab hold of it, pulling himself and the trolley onto the path beside the river.

‘Oh, thank you so much, you saved me, any longer in that mud, and I would have drowned, the names Tricia, Tricia Trolley.’

‘Nice to meet you, Tricia, my name is Cornelius, Cornelius Cone, I think we saved each other, I was about to go under, so that makes us even.’

‘How did you end up in the river Cornelius?’

‘I was working on the side of the road, looking after a newly repaired pothole, ’It can get dangerous, especially for the road workers, anyway, I was blown off the road by a fast-moving car,

I rolled down a hill into the river, how did you end up here, Tricia?’

‘Well, I used to work in a supermarket, I enjoyed being pushed, I loved carrying all kinds of things, but one day, I developed a wonky wheel, once you get a wonky wheel, you no longer get pushed into the supermarket.’ ‘I was outside in the cold rain, and to make things worse, one night, I was taken for a joy ride, then ended up being thrown into the river.’

‘I know what you mean, a friend of mine was taken one night, I looked everywhere for him, I eventually found him on top of a lamppost, he was not a happy chappie, but he is doing fine now, some cones can end up worse.’

‘Do you miss the supermarket Tricia?’

‘Of course, especially Wet Floor, he's a sort of cone too, his job is to stand next to puddles and spillages so that nobody would slip up, Wet Floor made me laugh; he told me funny jokes, I grew very fond of him, I do miss him.’

Tricia looked at Cornelius,

‘Umm, Cornelius is quite a long name; can I just call you Corny?’

‘Of course, you can, no problem Tricia.’

Moments pass, Cornelius, and Tricia begin to dry out in the sunshine,

‘OK, let's have a look at your wheel, perhaps I could see what is making it go wonky.’

‘Oh thank you, Corny that would be so nice of you.’

Cornelius looked closer at her wheel; he could see a long piece of string wrapped tightly around the wheel; this was the reason why it was wonky and needed to be pulled out.

Cornelius tried to pull the string from her wheel, but he did not have the strength to pull it free, it was stuck for sure.

‘I think we will need to get help; your wheel is so jammed up with string, I don’t have the strength to pull it out, perhaps we will find some help beyond this river; I will push you?’

Cornelius reached out to push Tricia Trolley, with a twiddle and a twiddle, it was not easy pushing her with a wonky wheel, but he tried his best to steer her as straight as he could along the river path.

‘So, where were you born Corny?’

‘I am not sure, my parents told me that I came from a recycling plant, but I never did find out where that plant was in the garden, I have been wondering all my life about where I was born.’

They follow the path until they meet a rubbish bin.

‘Hello, have you got any rubbish? I'm starving.’

‘Sorry, but we don't have any rubbish on us, why don't you join us. I am sure we will find some on the ground here and there.’

‘Thanks, but I am not allowed to move from here, besides, I cannot feed myself very well, I normally wait here for rubbish to be fed to me, oh, so sorry, my name is Bertie, Bertie bin.’

‘Pleased to meet you, Bertie, come on, come with us, we can feed rubbish to you on the way.’

‘Well, I guess nobody will even know I have gone from here anyway, let's face it, you are the only ones who have even seen me, I sometimes think I am invisible, I rarely get fed rubbish while I’m here.’

‘Sorry Corny, but who were you talking to?’

‘See what I mean?’

‘Oh come on Bertie, I was only joking, please join us.’

‘OK, why not, I should have done this long ago.’

They follow the path for a while, admiring the pleasant countryside, picking up the occasional discarded sweet wrapper to feed Bertie, Cornelius finds a plastic bottle and tries to put it into Bertie’s mouth.

‘No, not plastic bottles, I hate plastic bottles, I cannot digest them, Burp.’

Cornelius takes the plastic bottle and gives it to Tricia Trolley.

‘Here Tricia, we can put all the plastic bottles in your trolley, and clean up this place along the way.’

‘What are we going to do with all these bottles if you can’t eat them, Bertie?’

‘Well, I know a place that can turn those plastic bottles into amazing things; it's what is called a recycling plant.’

Cornelius stopped in his tracks, then turned to Bertie.

‘Are you telling me that a recycling plant is a place, Bertie?’

‘Yes, it's where they take my rubbish when I have eaten it.’

As they walk further along the path, they turn a corner and are shocked to see a massive pile of rubbish on the side of the path.

'Oh, who could dump this here in this beautiful countryside Bertie?'

'This is what they call 'fly-tipping,' it is usually dumped by thoughtless people who would instead drop it here than to take it to their local tip; we need to get it cleaned up.' 'I can eat most of the paper, there are more plastic bottles here, oh, I can also see a sofa, but that will be far too big to go in Tricia's trolley, and would have to be picked up another time.'

A moment later, they hear a voice cry out.

'Help, can you please help me?'

Cornelius moves closer to the pile of rubbish; the voice was coming from the bottom of the pile.

‘Careful Corny, it looks dangerous, you could get hurt; you never know what horrible things are dumped there.’

Cornelius approached with care, grabbed some rubbish, then gave it to Bertie, with a chomp, chomp, burpity chomp, Bertie swallowed all he could. They made their way through the pile, placing the plastic bottles into Tricia Trolley.

Moments later, they see a little hand waving at them through the pile of rubbish.

‘Here I am, quick, pull my hand.’

Cornelius reached out to the little hand and pulled with all his might, and to his amazement, he pulled out a Microwave.

‘Thank you ever so much; the name’s Mike.’

‘Pleased to meet you, Mike, what are you doing out here, shouldn't you be in a kitchen?’

‘Yes, about that, I was thrown out, I was a wonderful cook in my early days, but as I got older, I lost my ding, nobody could tell if my food was ready.’

‘We are off to find a recycling plant,’ said Cornelius, ‘perhaps if you come with us, we might be able to get your ding fixed.’

‘That would be great; I could do with a good clean.’

So Cornelius Cone, Tricia Trolley, Bertie Bin, and Mike Microwave follow the path toward a town.

A few moments later, they reach the end of the path, to a busy road on the edge of the town, over the road; they can see a huge building,

‘Yes, cried Bertie, ‘that is the recycling plant I was telling you about, quick, let's go.’

Just as they begin to cross the road, a loud voice calls to them.

‘STOP! It is dangerous to cross the road without pressing this button. You could get hit by traffic’.

‘Once you press this button, you will have to wait until my display changes to walk; then you will hear a beep, beep beep.

‘When it is safe to cross.’ ‘You will have to keep looking both ways until you reach the other side of the road, my name is Trevor, Trevor traffic light, I am here to make sure you get over the busy road safely.’

‘Oh hello Trevor, thank you very much, we got so excited about where we wanted to go, we forgot about the dangerous road.’

Cornelius pressed the button, the traffic stopped short of the crossing, the display changed from ‘Wait’ to ‘Walk’; then they heard the beep, beep, beep, looking both ways, they began to cross to the other side of the road, they waved at Trevor, thanking him again.

Once inside the building, they are greeted by a man in overalls, a hard hat and high visibility vest, Bertie walked up to him.

‘Hello, we have brought you all this rubbish to be recycled, we found a lot of plastic bottles too.’

‘Thank you very much; you have done well; let me help you sort this lot out, plastic bottles can be recycled, they can go here on this big conveyor belt, the paper goes over there on another conveyor belt and Microwave, this gentleman will take you to our repair room.’

Another member of staff looked down at Tricia's wonky wheel, he then grabs the end of the string, with a heave and a heave, the string is free from her wonky wheel.

‘Oh Corny, my wheel is fixed, I am so happy, I am on a roll, thank you very much, I will be able to go back into the supermarket to see Wet Floor again.’

Bertie begins to give his rubbish to the hard-working recyclers, who sort out the rubbish onto a conveyor belt, they take the plastic bottles from Tricia, and place them onto another conveyor belt, leading to a huge machine.

Cornelius then rushed to the other side of the machine, where he saw two cones with smiling faces, waiting with excitement for what will come out.

With a squeak and a squish, a plip, and a plop, the machine produces a small baby cone; the happy cones greet the baby cone with tears of joy.

Cornelius smiles as one of the cones pick up the baby cone, to hold it in their arms.

With a small tear in his eye, Cornelius watched as the two cones walk away from the recycling plant. He has finally found out where he was born.

Just then, the door to the other room opens, and there stood Mike, shining good as new.

‘I feel brand new again, and what's more, I have my ding back again.’ ding, ding, ding.

The recycler man walks up to give something to Bertie.

'Here, follow these directions, they will lead you to the park, once you get there, look for Bella, she will take care of you.'

Feeling very proud that they have made a difference, Cornelius, Tricia, Bertie, and Mike thank the recycling plant staff and go on their way.

They walk down the street; Mike stops outside an electrical store, he decides that this is where he should say his goodbyes.

‘This is me guys; it has been nice knowing you, thanks for everything, this place will find me a new home, now I have my ding again, I will not have to wait long, I will keep in touch.’

He gives a little wave as he passes through the door.

Tricia, Cornelius, and Bertie continue down the street, following the directions they had been given at the recycling plant, in no time at all, they reach the entrance to the park.

As they enter the gates to the park; they see Bella, a bright green recycling bin, Bertie walks over to greet her; she takes hold of Bertie's hand.

‘Stay here with me; we can work together; this is a lovely place. We never go hungry here.’

Bertie looks back at Cornelius Tricia and Mike.

‘I will stay here now; this is where I should be, it has been a pleasure meeting you, come and visit us sometime. Goodbye for now.’

‘Goodbye, Bertie, and thank you; we will.’

It was lovely to see Bertie and Bella, standing next to each other holding hands they, look like they were made for each other.

Cornelius then began to push Tricia out of the park and down the street, until they reach the supermarket, Tricia tells him to put her in the trolley space.

'Well, this is it, Tricia, I hope things turn out well for you, it has been a real pleasure, we helped clean up the countryside, and made a few friends on our way.'

‘Thanks for everything Corny, I will never forget you, visit the supermarket some time, and I will introduce you to Wet Floor .’

‘I look forward to that Tricia. See you then.’

He slowly walks away, and as he turns to wave at her, he can see Tricia being pushed inside the supermarket, with a huge smile on her face.

Cornelius then begins his journey out of the town.

As he walks away from the town, he could see a Bollard struggling to get upright. Cornelius rushed over to the bollard to help pull him upright.

To his surprise, he could see it was a friend he had not seen for a while.

‘Billy Bollard, is that you?’

‘Hello Cornelius, so good to see you, buddy, thanks ever so much for the help, what brings you here, it’s been a long time?’

‘It certainly has been; I am trying to get back to the country road, I hope I am going in the right direction.’

‘Well this is the only road out of town, so it seems you are going the right way.’

‘Thanks, Billy, I wish we had more time to chat, but I have to get back to the country road; I don’t want to miss my ride home.’

‘Ok Cornelius, mind how you go, the path runs out along this road, there are a lot of potholes too, we don’t want you to fall down one, it was good to see you again, bye.’

Cornelius waved at Billy and continued down the road, just as Billy said, the pathway had ended, so he had to be extra careful, listening and looking for traffic.

After a while, he reached his destination, exactly where he began his adventure, just in time to see the Maintenance truck arriving to take him home.

'Hello Cornelius, time to go, how was your day?'

Printed in Great Britain
by Amazon

41586960R00022